LEMON TARTS AND FIERY DARTS

A Sandy Bay Cozy Mystery

By

Amber Crewes

For questions and comments about this book, please contact info@ambercrewes.com

www.AmberCrewes.com

ISBN: 9781095328514
Imprint: Independently Published

Lemon Tarts and Fiery Darts

Other books in the Sandy Bay Series

A

Sandy Bay

COZY MYSTERY

Book Twelve

Amber Crewes

1

MEGHAN TRUMAN'S HEART WAS POUNDING in her chest as she turned on her laptop computer. Her fingers hovered above the keys for a moment as Meghan held her breath, and as the screen loaded, she felt her face grow hot.

"What if it is not what I wanted?" she thought to herself as the page opened. "What if I am disappointed?

Just then, Pamela, Meghan's teenage employee, tapped her on the shoulder. Pamela had been working at Truly Sweet, the bakery Meghan owned, for nearly six months, and Meghan adored her company.

"Hey, is it ready?" Pamela asked, her eyes wide.

She shook her head, tucking a stray lock of dark, wavy hair behind her ear as she squinted at the screen. "The web designer said it would take a few minutes to open…"

Pamela giggled. "I think your computer might just be a little slow," she told Meghan. "It looks like it is a million years old."

Meghan rolled her eyes playfully. "It's almost as old as you," she teased Pamela. "I got a great deal on it a few years ago, and I've grown fond of this little computer. It isn't fancy, but it does the job."

Pamela grinned. "I just can't wait to see it," she cried. "I've never had my picture on a website before. Thank you for letting me be your model with the bakery's new website!"

Meghan smiled. "You were the perfect choice," she told Pamela. "The designer told me that we needed some shots of a customer eating our treats, and I would rather hire you, my friend, rather than a model. The pictures were adorable, too, and I think they will add so much to our social media presence."

"I wish you had been in more pictures," Pamela told Meghan. "We could have taken some cute ones together."

Meghan laughed. "I'm not one for photos," she told Pamela. "Besides, you are young and fresh. Your pretty face on the website will certainly help us out."

"Young and fresh? Meghan Truman, you are twenty-eight years old. You are still young and certainly still fresh, whatever that means."

Meghan chuckled as Trudy, another employee, joined the conversation. Trudy was old enough to be Meghan's mother, but her biting sarcasm and wit kept Meghan laughing, and she enjoyed having Trudy around.

"Thanks, Trudy," she blushed. "And Pamela, there are some pictures of me on the website. Don't you worry, Sandy Bay will get plenty of Meghan Truman."

"You mean the world," Pamela interrupted. "It's the World Wide Web, Meghan. Millions of people could see the new website, not just people in Sandy Bay."

"Oh, look," Trudy squealed as the page finally loaded. "It's ready! The new website is ready."

Meghan gasped as the page opened, thrilled with what she saw. The new bakery logo was at the top of the page, the bakery's name written in gold cursive lettering. The website had a whimsical feel to it; on every page were staged and candid photos of Pamela enjoying treats, and the story of the bakery's beginnings included pictures of Meghan, Trudy, and Pamela.

"Look at us," Pamela shrieked joyfully as she pointed to a picture of the trio playfully licking bright pink frosting off their fingers. "We look so cute."

"Yes, we do," she agreed, pleased that her investment had lived up to her expectations.

Nearly a year ago, Meghan had left behind a life in Los Angeles to follow her friend, Karen, to Sandy Bay, a small town in the Pacific Northwest. Karen, a native of Sandy Bay, had assured her that the town would be the perfect place for a fresh start. Meghan had fulfilled her dream of opening the bakery, and before her eyes, her business had bloomed; Truly Sweet was one of the most popular bakeries in the Pacific Northwest, and Meghan's professional life was thriving so much that she had decided to hire a website designer to upgrade her social media presence, and now, as she gazed at her rebranded website, she was elated to have made the investment.

Her personal life in Sandy Bay was also thriving; after a few months of getting to know each other, Jack Irvin, a handsome police officer, had asked her to be his girlfriend. Jack had been promoted to a detective, and she was proud to be dating an upstanding member of society. Jack had met her parents during the holidays, and they had grown to adore the man that Meghan had fallen in love with.

Meghan was genuinely happy in Sandy Bay; despite a few obstacles in her first few months of living in the small town, she had made great friends, fallen in love, and created a business from the ground up.

Meghan turned her attention back to the website, eager to see more of its features. "How do we access our other social media accounts?" she asked Pamela.

"There is a link to our Instagram account in the bottom

of the page," Pamela told Meghan. "Why don't you click on it? I've been uploading some great content over the last few days to match the aesthetic of the new page, and I think you will like it."

Meghan clicked the button and was redirected to Instagram, a website and application that allowed visitors to share images. Her jaw dropped as she opened the page she had asked Pamela to create for the bakery. The account was filled with bright, filtered pictures of the bakery, the staff, and the various treats for sale. The colors and layouts of the photos matched the vision that she had had for the bakery website, and Meghan was thrilled that the website and the Instagram went together perfectly.

"Pamela, this is absolutely adorable," Meghan gushed as she clicked through the perfectly curated gallery of images.

"Look how many followers we have," Pamela beamed. "Five thousand followers, Meghan. Five thousand people are following our accounts and seeing our pictures."

Meghan's eyes glistened with tears. She had the best employees, and she was thankful that Pamela had taken the time to create the Instagram account.

"I think we need to update our Facebook, too," Trudy chimed in. "We older gals like Facebook more than that instaphoto, or whatever it's called. Can we use some of the popular photos on the Instagram to post on our Facebook?"

Meghan smiled. "Of course," she said.

"Our pictures of the lemon tarts have been getting a ton of likes," Pamela added. "Let's use that."

Trudy wrinkled her nose. "Oh, really? The lemon tart photos? That's interesting. Someone in this town must be in love with our lemon tarts, because not only have those photos been receiving the most attention, but they have been receiving a lot of orders. We've had nearly a hundred lemon tart orders in the last week!"

Meghan raised an eyebrow. "Nearly a hundred orders of lemon tarts? Are you serious?"

"That doesn't surprise me."

Meghan swiveled in her chair at the familiar sound of Jack's voice. He was standing in the doorway grinning, his blue eyes bright with excitement. Her heart beat faster as she smiled at her handsome boyfriend. He was dressed in his detective's uniform, his badges shining in the light of the dining room.

"Hi, babe," she said, standing up to embrace her boyfriend. "This is a surprise!"

"I had a little break and wanted to stop by," Jack said as he bent down to kiss her on the nose.

"What were you saying about the tarts?" Meghan said

as Jack stepped back and settled onto the top of a little white table. "It's so weird that someone ordered so many; we usually don't sell more than fifteen each month…"

Jack mischievously winked at Meghan. "Let's just say that Detective Irvin may have the scoop, and the scoop is pretty darn interesting" he teased as she shook her head in amusement.

2

THE NEXT DAY, Meghan decided to make a visit to the local library. It was a chilly spring day in Sandy Bay, and she unhappily slipped her winter coat on over her sweater; despite the sunshine, it was a bitterly cold day in the Pacific Northwest, and Meghan was in need of some warmth after the harsh winter.

"Fiesta, Siesta," she called out to her little twin dogs who were resting comfortably on her bed. "Mama is going to the library. I'll be back in a little bit to take you for a walk."

The dogs barked good-naturedly at Meghan, and she blew them a kiss as she shut her bedroom door. She walked out of her apartment, locking the door before descending the stairs. She entered the bakery, waved hello to Trudy and Pamela, and then left, shivering as the wind struck her cheeks.

Despite the cold, the walk to the library was pleasant; Meghan enjoyed the sound of the Pacific Ocean, and she never took for granted the town's close proximity to the sea. The salty air always made Meghan excited for the summertime, and she envisioned herself spending the summer afternoons picnicking with Jack, or strolling alongside the shore with her dogs.

"Welcome to the library," a bespectacled librarian greeted Meghan as she walked inside.

"Thank you," she whispered in reply.

Meghan wandered to the technology section. She had been so pleased with her new website and Pamela's work on the social media pages that she wanted to be able to contribute. After spending a few hours in the morning researching different types of web design approaches, Meghan had been stumped; she was not very savvy with social media or technology, and she knew she needed to learn as much as she could in order to help her business thrive. She could not afford to hire a designer each time she wanted to make an update to her website, and she was determined to teach herself how to navigate the internet.

As Meghan scanned the titles of the technology books, she became lost in her thoughts; she imagined the bakery's popularity expanding even more than it had in the last year, and she grinned as she perused the section. Suddenly, she felt a sharp jab in her side, and she yelped in pain.

"Ouch!"

"Sorry, I didn't see you there."

She turned to see Chief Nunan, the head of the Sandy Bay Police. Chief Nunan had a stack of books at her feet, and Meghan hastily apologized. "I didn't mean to make you drop your books, Chief," she lamented. "So sorry. I was daydreaming, and I ran right into you."

Chief Nunan shrugged. "It happens," she told Meghan. "But don't let it happen again, or I'll have to take you downtown."

Her eyes widened at the threat, but when she realized the chief was only joking, she giggled. "Yes, ma'am," she said, playing along with the chief. "What brings you into the library today, Chief?"

The Chief smiled. "Well, besides being run into by unruly citizens, I came here to look for a book on the law," she explained. "There's a case in my queue right now that I have some questions about, and I need to learn more."

Meghan nodded. "I'm in the same boat," she said. "Well, sort of. I need to find a book for work."

"A cookbook?" Chief Nunan asked.

Meghan shook her head. "No," she said. "A book about the internet."

Chief Nunan chuckled. "Are you selling treats online?"

Meghan laughed. "Not quite," she told her. "I hired a

designer to revamp my website, and I feel like I need to know how to make the updates myself," she explained. "Pamela, my employee, keeps talking about SEO, and I have no idea what SEO even is. I think it's a website thing, but I'm a little embarrassed that I don't know."

Chief Nunan patted her shoulder. "It's perfectly okay to not know everything," she told Meghan. "In fact, it's admirable that you are going out of your way to learn more in order to help your business."

Meghan blushed. "Thanks," she said to the Chief. "I just want to be a well-rounded businesswoman."

"You are well on your way," the Chief commended her. "Just be patient with yourself. And, if you can't figure out SEO, and all of that other internet stuff, come down to the station sometime. We have an IT guy who is a tech genius. Seriously, he knows his stuff, Meghan. I could set up a meeting between the pair of you. What do you think?"

Meghan grinned. "That is so nice of you to offer," she gushed.

"Anytime," Chief Nunan told her. "I need to get back to the station, but I hope you enjoy your time at the library, Meghan. I'll tell that detective of yours you said hello."

"Please do," she said, her cheeks growing red at the mention of her boyfriend.

Meghan waved goodbye to the chief, and then turned back to the bookshelf. "Hmmm," she murmured to herself as she looked through a row of thick, intimidating books. "I don't think I'll find something that will help turn me into a computer pro. These books are huge. I could spend my whole life thumbing through them and never know enough."

Meghan glanced down and saw exactly what she needed, feeling as though divine intervention had somehow placed the perfect book in her path. "SEO and Internet Use for Dopes" she read, laughing at the irreverent title. "This is perfect for me."

"Dopes, huh?"

Meghan was startled to find a man staring at her from a few feet away. She hadn't noticed his arrival, but it was clear that he had been watching her. He looked to be Meghan's age, and he was quite handsome; with his sharp jaw, broad shoulders, and tall stature, she could not help but to notice how attractive he was.

"Hey," she said kindly. "How's it going?"

The man sneered. "I'm cracking up watching you talk to yourself," he said haughtily, his green eyes dancing. "Do you always do that? Is it a dope thing, because if it is, you have the perfect book."

Meghan's jaw dropped. She was in awe of the man's rudeness. She no longer cared if he was handsome; she was put off by his terrible manners.

"Excuse me?" she asked, crossing her arms in front of her chest. "What was that?"

"Nothing," the man said with a shrug. "I didn't say anything at all."

The man turned and strutted out of the library, his head held high. Meghan was repulsed by his arrogance, and embarrassed by the encounter. "That's the last time I come to the library," she muttered as she hung her head and left.

3

MEGHAN LEFT THE LIBRARY AND DECIDED to stop by the grocery store; she was running low on Geos, her favorite potato chips, and she wanted a snack to enjoy as she thumbed through her new library books. She breathed in a sigh of relief as she entered the grocery store. Unlike the library, where she rarely ventured, in the grocery, a place where food and treats were sold and displayed, she felt right at home.

Meghan found the chips, and then wandered into the baked goods section. She bent down to examine the sugar shelf, intrigued to see a new brand of coconut sugar being sold.

"Meghan Truman! What a nice surprise to see you here."

She turned to find Otis Barber smiling at her, his smile wide. Otis was one of Sandy Bay's most celebrated residents; along with working at Fit Miss, a women's only gym in town, Otis was known for his generosity and commitment to the community. He frequently volunteered at the Lads and Ladies Club, the free after-school program for low-come families, and he had founded the Sandy Bay Less Large League, a motivational weight-loss program for locals that focused on transforming one's inside, as well as the outside. Karen Denton, Meghan's dear friend, was a close friend of Otis, and Meghan had always enjoyed his shy, but warm nature.

"How is it going, Otis?" she asked, happy to see a familiar face smiling back at her. "What are you up to today?"

Otis grinned. "It's cheat day," he told her. "One day a week, the Sandy Bay Less Large League sponsors an official cheat day. Members are encouraged to disregard their diets and focus on eating things that make them happy. Today, I was craving a donut, so here I am."

Meghan nodded. "I would cheat for donuts any day," she teased.

Otis winked. "I'll let you take one, if you'd like."

Meghan shook her head. "I'm just kidding," she said. "Although, how perfect it is that I ran into you at the grocery store. Karen and I were visiting last week, and she mentioned that you have the best curry recipe in the world. I've never tried curry, but she ranted and raved about yours. I think I am curious. What is in your recipe?"

Otis beamed. "I am so happy she said that," he told her. "The curry recipe I use came from my grandmother, Kathryn. She lived in India during her childhood, and she passed the recipe down to my father. The recipe calls for a sprinkling of basil, which is not typically used, and I think that is what gives it its unique taste."

Meghan whipped out her phone and gestured at Otis. "Could you text the recipe to me? I think I need to try it. I love basil, and I have been saying that it is time I expand my cooking expertise."

Otis took her phone and typed the recipe. "There you go," he said upon finishing. "I hope you enjoy it. Anything else I can do for you, Ms. Truman?"

Meghan raised her eyebrows. "Actually, there is," she agreed. "Karen also told me that you have a killer Zumba DVD that I should borrow from you. There's no way you have it on you, do you?"

Otis shook his head, and she marveled at his height and bulk. At nearly seven feet tall and three-hundred pounds, Otis was built like a horse. Meghan giggled to herself as she imagined Otis doing Zumba.

"What are you laughing about?" Otis teased.

"I was just thinking about you doing Zumba," she confessed.

"Don't hate on Zumba," Otis pretended to chastise her.

"When I played junior hockey in Canada, my team did Zumba every day; my coaches swore that Zumba was what made us so agile and flexible."

"You played professional hockey?" she asked. "That is so cool."

"It was fun while it lasted," Otis shrugged. "Anyway, one of my friends is borrowing the DVD, but when she gives it back, I'll be happy to lend it to you."

"Thanks!" she chirped, imagining herself dancing in her apartment. "I'm a good borrower, I promise."

Otis' face darkened. "What's wrong?" she asked.

Otis frowned. "You know who is a terrible borrower?" he asked Meghan. "Chandler Washington. He's my neighbor, and he's constantly borrowing things and bringing them back broken."

She crossed her arms in front of her chest. "That's annoying," she affirmed. "Bad borrowers are the worst."

Otis scowled. "I hate to complain about anyone," he said to Meghan. "But man, that guy thinks he is the cat's pajamas. Give a guy an IT degree and he thinks he is a gift to the world."

"I will make sure I don't borrow anything from him," she told Otis. "I'm sorry he's an annoying neighbor."

Otis returned to his pleasant manner. "I'm sorry I vented," he apologized. "It's just all been adding up. Anyway, I have to run. I am teaching a Pilates class tonight, and I need to go. It was good to see you, Meghan."

"Good to see you, Otis," she said, in awe as she leaned over to give Otis a side hug and was met with a wall of pure muscle. "See you later!"

Back at her apartment, Meghan removed her winter coat and climbed into her bed. Fiesta and Siesta cuddled at her feet, and she pulled Siesta onto her chest and began to scratch his ears. Her phone rang, and she answered it, happy to see Jack's name on the screen.

"What are you up to, babe?" Jack asked in a cheerful voice.

"I just got home from the store," she said. "I ran into Otis Barber."

"He is such a good guy," Jack told her. "He was a few years older than me in school, but he was always nice to me when we played football together."

"That doesn't surprise me," she replied. "Anyway, what's up with you, babe?"

"I need to ask a favor," he said. "It's not too crazy, but it would be so helpful."

"What can I do for you?"

"I know it's last minute," he began. "But do you think you could bring some lemon tarts over to the station? We're celebrating Officer Green's retirement, and he loves your lemon tarts."

Meghan looked at her watch. She did not know if she had a surplus of lemon tarts, and she was not sure she could whip up a batch as quickly as Jack needed them.

"Beautiful?"

"Sorry, I was trying to figure out how many I have," she told him.

"We only need a few; we're celebrating at the station, and then moving the party to one of the bars. Officer Green wants to play darts, and I think we're going to do a showdown between the officers and tech folks."

Meghan bit her lip. She was so cozy as she relaxed in her bed, and she had no desire to venture back out into the cold night.

"Please, Meghan?" he asked. "Officer Bradley was my mentor when I first came to the station. I know it is a lot to ask of you, and I probably should have asked you sooner, but it would mean so much to me if I could bring his favorite treat."

"I'll do it," she answered immediately, hearing the urgency in Jack's voice. She knew her boyfriend hardly made demands and she sensed this request really meant a lot to him. "I'll make it work."

4

MEGHAN STARED AT HER REFLECTION, smiling as she surveyed the curls she had twirled into her long, dark hair with the new curling iron her mother had sent her for Christmas. She ran a hand through her locks, hoping to loosen the curls so they looked more natural.

"Jack has never seen my hair like this," she thought to herself as she admired the way the ringlets framed her face. "I hope he likes it."

Meghan had spent nearly an hour preparing for the retirement party. She typically didn't spend too much time on her appearance, but tonight, she wanted to make a good impression; she knew Jack liked to show her off to his colleagues, and Meghan was excited to look her best.

"Fiesta, Siesta, what should I wear?" she muttered as her dogs slept on the bed. "Should I put on heels for tonight? What about a dress?"

She remembered that the retirement party was at the

bar, but with so many people coming, she figured that the attendees would dress up in honor of Officer Green. Meghan selected a green long-sleeve dress from her closet and laid it out on the bed. She smoothed the skirt, which fell just above her knees.

"I'll need those stockings with these," she decided as she turned to her dresser. Meghan rummaged through the drawers and chose a pair of gray tights. "This will look great with the silver necklace Jack got for me for Valentine's Day," she exclaimed, opening her jewelry box and removing the long double-stranded silver necklace.

When Meghan finished dressing, she tucked her hair behind her ears and gave herself one final inspection. "My hair needs another round of curling," she decided, taking her curling iron out of its box and turning it back on.

As she gathered a strand of hair and began to weave it through the curling iron, she dropped it. The hot iron hit her knee, and then bounced onto the floor and hitting her foot. "Ouch!" she yelled, waking the dogs. "I burned myself! What a clutz I am."

Meghan bit her lip and bent down to pick up the curling iron. She was dismayed to find that her stocking had a large, angry black burn mark. "I ruined my tights," she lamented as she pulled them off of her legs and tossed them into the trash can. "Now I am going to have to redo my entire outfit."

Forty-five minutes later, Meghan arrived at the bar. She had never been to this bar before; she knew it was a place that the police officers frequented on weeknights, and she was eager to see the place Jack spent his Wednesday evenings watching professional hockey with his friends on the squad.

She applied a layer of fresh mauve lipstick and turned off her car. She got out, and opened the passenger seat to retrieve the two boxes of lemon tarts she had scrounged up from the kitchen. Before she could close the car door, she lost her footing, and before she knew it, one box of tarts lay on the icy ground in front of her.

"No!" Meghan cried as she looked at the mess of broken treats before her. "What is wrong with me? Why am I so graceless lately?"

She cleaned up the mess, thankful that the second box of tarts was salvageable. She took a deep breath, adjusted her hair, and walked into the bar, trying her best to smile.

"Meghan!" Jack called out as she walked inside. She looked at him in horror. Jack was dressed in jeans and a ratty t-shirt he usually wore to wash Dash, his dog. Meghan glanced around the room, her face burning as she realized everyone was dressed casually. Even Chief Nunan was out of her uniform; she had a pair of black sweatpants on, and her hair was tied up in a messy ponytail.

"You're sure dressed up," Jack commented as the color rose to Meghan's face. "Didn't I tell you that this party was low-key?"

Meghan nodded. "You did," she admitted, feeling self-conscious about her overdressed appearance. "But I must have forgotten…"

Jack grinned. "You are the prettiest girl here by a longshot," he told her. "I like that you dressed up, babe. You always look beautiful."

Meghan smiled, thankful for her sweet boyfriend. "Thanks, Jack," she said. "Here, I brought a box of lemon tarts."

"Awesome!" he exclaimed, taking the box from Meghan's hands. "Let me take these to the refreshment table, and then I'll show you around. You know most of my coworkers already, but I'm sure everyone wants to say hello to you."

Jack led Meghan to a table filled with food. He carefully set the box of tarts onto the table. "Thanks again for bringing these," he said to Meghan as he leaned over to kiss her cheek.

"Anything for you," she replied, fluttering her eyelashes at her boyfriend.

"Irvin! Is that your pretty girlfriend? You are sure out kicking your coverage, man!"

Meghan and Jack turned to find Officer Green grinning at them. He was a large man, taller than Jack, and his grey hair was cut close to his head. He had dark blue eyes with deep smile lines cut below, and he smiled happily at Meghan.

"Out kicking your coverage?" she whispered to Jack. "What does that mean?"

"It means that you are way out of my league," Jack told her with a wink. "And I agree!"

"Thank you for coming to my retirement party," Officer Green said to Meghan. "I'm so glad you could join us, and Jacky-boy here said that you brought lemon tarts?"

"I did," she confirmed, nodding her chin at the refreshment table. "Jack mentioned that they are your favorite, and I whipped up a quick batch this afternoon."

"Fantastic," Officer Green replied. "I hope you enjoy my little shindig, Meghan. It was a difficult decision to leave the Sandy Bay Police and settle into retirement, but this last-hoorah will be a nice goodbye to my friends and coworkers. My wife planned the party, and she told me over fifty people came out to celebrate. Can you believe it?"

She peered around the crowded bar. Giant televisions hung in each corner, and loud country music was blaring over the speakers. Meghan saw many familiar faces, and she smiled and waved as she made eye contact with Cheryl, Officer Green's wife.

"This is a big turnout," Meghan praised as Officer Green blushed. "You've done so much for the community, Officer. I know Jack looks up to you so much. What an honor it is to celebrate you."

Before Officer Green could reply, an obnoxiously loud voice filled the bar. "SCORE! HIGH SCORE!"

Meghan, Jack, and Officer Green turned around. "It's that Chandler Washington," Officer Green muttered as Meghan saw a man in a loud orange t-shirt across the room pumping his fist, a dart in one hand and a beer in the other. "That kid has no idea when to shut his mouth. I wish I could have not invited him, but Cheryl said I couldn't leave out someone from the office…"

Meghan's heart sank. She realised that Chandler Washington was the rude fellow from the library. She felt her face grow hot as she recalled how nasty he had been, and she understood why so many people seemed irritated with him.

"He doesn't seem to know when to be quiet," she agreed quietly. "He was really rude to me at the library the other day."

Officer Green's face darkened. "That punk was rude to you? Jack Irvin's girl? I'm not going to let that stand. I'm gonna go tell that kid to be quiet. I don't care if he is winning his dart game; I don't want to hear his loud voice for another minute."

Meghan stared as Officer Green marched over to Chandler. "He really seems to dislike him," she said to Jack.

Jack nodded. "He's a problem at the office," he told Meghan. "He's unruly and crass, and no one really likes him."

"I can see that Officer Green isn't a fan," Meghan confirmed as she watched Officer Green point a finger in Chandler's face.

"That's for sure," Jack agreed. "There's some tension at the office between the police staff and the IT crew; the IT crew makes double what the officers make, and it seems like the officers keep getting slashes to their paychecks while the IT group keeps getting raises. The IT group also seem to have terrible attitudes most of the time, and they don't like to lend a hand to the officers."

Meghan shook her head. "That sounds frustrating," she said.

Suddenly, there was a commotion by the dart board. "If you aren't gonna leave, then I guess we'll start the darts competition now," she heard Officer Green declare. "If we win, then you've gotta go, Chandler."

She saw a smirk on Chandler's face. "This seems like trouble," she murmured to Jack, her dark eyes wide.

The crowd rushed over to the dart board, and the two teams huddled together. The IT team, led by Chandler, fist-bumped, cackling as they picked up their darts and went to their spots. The team of officers, led by Officer Green, solemnly assumed their positions as the game began.

"If you don't stop that laughing, Chandler, I'm going to strike you with one of these darts," Officer Green shouted over the music as the game began."

Chandler puffed up his chest and rolled his eyes. "You're retiring, old man," he laughed as Officer Green glared at him. "Why don't you save your energy for some shuffleboard?" Or maybe get a cane to help you with your darts game?" Officer Green glowered at Chandler. He picked up a red-tailed dart, and the game began.

"I'm sorry it was a little crazy at the party tonight," Jack apologized as he walked Meghan to her car. "I didn't expect Officer Green to get so fired up. He really let Chandler get to him, didn't he?"

Meghan shook her head. "It was one thing when they were fighting early in the night, but Officer Green was so upset when Chandler and the IT guys won the darts tournament."

Jack sighed. "Officer Green gets intense," he admitted. "I'm sorry you had to see that. I can't believe he spoke to Chandler like that."

Meghan frowned. "It didn't seem right for a police officer to be threatening someone," she said to Jack. "When Officer Green threatened to kill Chandler after the IT guys won the darts game, I was pretty upset."

"Retired police officer," Jack corrected playfully. "Anyway, let's just pretend like we didn't hear it. It was his retirement party, and we want to remember Officer Green in a good light. Remember, he was my mentor, Meghan. I know he messed up tonight in the way he treated Chandler, but he's a good guy. I really look up to him, even after what he said."

Meghan nodded. "I understand," she said as Jack's phone began to ring. "We all mess up sometimes."

Jack held up a finger to indicate Meghan pause the conversation. He answered the phone call, and Meghan watched the color drain from his face. "Just now?" Jack asked. "Are you sure?"

She raised an eyebrow. "I'll be right there," Jack said, and then hung up the phone.

"What's wrong?" she asked, seeing the panicked look on Jack's face.

"It's Chandler," he replied.

"Chandler? What does that jerk want?" she asked.

"Nothing," Jack answered. "He's dead."

5

"I THINK OFFICER GREEN DID HIM IN," Trudy announced gravely as she, Pamela, and Meghan huddled together in the bakery, three cups of tea in front of them. "Meghan, you said Officer Green threatened to kill him after the game of darts? It sounds like he made good on that promise."

Pamela shook her head vigorously. "There's no way he did it," she insisted, her face wrought with worry. "Officer Green is such a nice man. When my grandmother fell down in her condo, he was the first to arrive on the scene. He helped her, and he was so sweet to her when she was scared and shaken up from her fall. There's no way he did it."

Trudy looked at Meghan. "You were at the bar last night before Chandler died," she said. "What do you think? Do you think Officer Green could be a killer?"

Meghan bit her bottom lip. She thought of how wound up Officer Green had been during the darts game, and how frightened she had been when he had gotten in

Chandler's face at the end of the evening. "I don't know," she admitted. "I would like to think not; Officer Green is a huge role model to Jack, and Jack is a good judge of character."

Trudy rolled her eyes. "You always see the best in people," she told Meghan.

"I think that's a good thing," Pamela declared. "Meghan gives people chances!"

Meghan shrugged, taking a sip of her chai tea. "It's not my place to say what happened," she told the ladies. "All I know is that Jack received a phone call only moments after it happened. He had to run back inside and get to work on the investigation. I've barely heard from him since we said goodbye last night, so I don't have any information besides what they have been saying on the news."

Pamela looked sternly at Trudy. "They are saying a dart killed him," she said. "And that Officer Green has a solid alibi."

Trudy sighed. "His wife is his alibi," she said. "That doesn't count; she's on his side."

Meghan held up her hands. "Let's stop speculating," she ordered. "This is a sad day; even if Chandler wasn't the nicest guy, it is sad that he died. We should be more respectful of the situation and stop talking about it so casually. Anyway, let's change the subject."

"I know what we should talk about," Pamela said. "We need to update our user options for our Instagram page, Meghan. Can you help with that? Since you are the owner of the bakery, I think you should make the decisions about the page."

Meghan's eyes widened. "Ummmm," she sputtered. "I checked out some books on SEO, but I thought Instagram was your area of expertise, Pamela?"

Pamela shook her head. "I'm only a teenager," she laughed good-naturedly. "I can't add the business information without your approval, Meghan."

Meghan nodded, her face turning red. "I think I will need some help with it," she admitted to Pamela and Trudy. "I know our internet marketing is important, and I want to grow the business. I need some support to do so. Chandler isn't available anymore, so...."

Pamela grinned. "Meghan, remember that day at the library? You said you bumped into Chief Nunan and she had a contact at the station who could help you!"

Meghan smiled. "You are right," she agreed. "She did say she had someone in mind. I am going to swing by the station later to drop off lunch for Jack...maybe Chief Nunan will point me in the direction of someone who can help with my tech needs."

A few hours later, Meghan ventured over to the Sandy Bay Police Station with a healthy meal she had prepared for Jack. She knew that with Chandler's death, he likely had not had a moment to rest or eat, and she made sure to include a variety of delicious treats in the package as well. She left the lunch on Jack's desk with a sweet love note attached, and then went to Chief Nunan's quarters.

"Chief?" Meghan said as she knocked on the door. The Chief answered, a grim look on her face.

"Jack isn't in here, Meghan," the Chief told her.

"I'm so sorry to bother you, but I have a question," she said.

"I haven't slept, and I have a meeting in ten minutes," the Chief sighed. "Please make it a quick question?"

Meghan nodded. "That day at the library," she began. "You mentioned an IT wizard here at the station. Can you point me in their direction? I need some help."

The Chief gestured with her chin toward the left. "Molly Owen," she answered. "Her office is right next door to the left. I think she's in there right now."

"Thanks," Meghan said as she ducked out of the office. "I'll get out of your hair."

Meghan walked to the door next to the Chief's and knocked. "Come in," a female's voice called. She stepped inside.

"Are you Molly?" she asked as the woman nodded.

"I'm sorry to bother you, but I was looking for an IT person, and Chief Nunan sang your praises."

Molly Owen smiled shyly, nervously twirling her strawberry blonde hair between her fingers. She had pale skin and a face filled with freckles, and Meghan thought she couldn't be any older than twenty-two years old.

"That was nice of her to say," Molly said softly. "Who are you, exactly? How can I help?"

Meghan smiled warmly. "I'm Meghan, Jack Irvin's girlfriend?"

"Oh, Jack," Molly nodded. "I'm new here, and Jack has been so nice. He showed me around the first day."

"He's a good guy," Meghan agreed. "That doesn't surprise me. Anyway, I'm having a little issue with my website and social media pages, and I need some assistance. I own and operate a bakery in town, and I'm trying to expand our internet marketing. Do you know anything about Instagram?"

Molly bobbed her head up and down. "Of course," she told Meghan. "Sit down with me, and we can chat."

An hour later, Meghan was feeling confident about her ability to manage her website and social media pages. Molly had explained the Instagram issue slowly and patiently, and she appreciated her gentle demeanor. "You are the best," she told Molly. "I would never have made it through this issue without you. You are so much better than some of the other IT people I've met."

"You mean Chandler?"

Meghan watched as Molly's face fell, and she knew she should not have made such a callous comment given Chandler's death. "Oh, Molly," she whispered. "I should not have said that."

Molly's eyes filled with tears. "I know that Chandler was hard to take," she admitted. "But he knew his stuff, Meghan. He also taught me a lot about coding and programming. I've been at the station just over a month, and he really took me under his wing professionally."

Meghan nodded. "I shouldn't have said anything," she repeated. "I didn't mean to be rude, Molly."

Molly wiped a tear from her green eyes. "It's okay," she said. "I get it. Chandler was not an easy guy to deal with, and I know how he could be."

Meghan forced a smile onto her face. "Let me make it up to you," she told Molly. "I didn't mean to upset you, and I want us to be friends. Why don't you stop by the bakery sometime? I owe you for your time today, and I would love to have you over for some desserts and tea. Please! It would be my treat! Literally!"

Molly laughed. "That would be truly sweet of you," she kidded as Meghan giggled. "Get it? Truly sweet!"

6

MEGHAN'S HEAD TURNED as she heard the little silver bells attached to the front door of Truly Sweet chime. She had only opened the bakery moments ago, and with the unexpected snowfall the night before, she was not expecting many customers as the road conditions were treacherous.

"Nice to see you, Meghan," Officer Green greeted her as he walked in the door with Cheryl, his wife.

Meghan was shocked to see Officer Green, and she dropped the cup of hot chocolate she was holding. "Oh no," she muttered as she tried to brush off the steaming liquid.

"Let me help you," Officer Green said as he rushed toward her.

"I'm okay," she insisted. "Give me just a moment, and then I will come help you."

Meghan fled to the back and removed her stained apron. She dabbed cold water onto her jeans, frowning as she examined the spill. "I am so clumsy," she lamented as she put on a fresh apron. "I just need to get myself together."

She returned to the dining area with a smile on her face. "All better now," she told Officer Green and Cheryl. "How many I help you today?"

Cheryl smiled at Meghan. "Two teas, please," she asked. "And perhaps a blueberry peppermint scone?"

Meghan nodded. "Of course."

Cheryl leaned up and kissed her husband on the lips. "Isn't it nice to be able to do this?" she asked Officer Green. "Tea dates in the morning together without any distractions? I've been looking forward to your retirement for the last two years, dear, and I'm looking forward to more quiet mornings like this together. No more sirens, no more emergencies, and no more late nights away from home."

Meghan's heart warmed as she watched Officer Green and Cheryl choose a table and sit down together. Officer Green slipped his hands across the table and take Cheryl's, and she imagined herself and Jack later in life, spending quality time together as they settled down and retired.

The little silver bells chimed again, tearing Meghan from her daydream. She looked up and was elated to see Jack and Officer Kim, one of his colleagues.

"Babe!" she cried joyfully. "What a surprise. What can I get for you?"

Officer Kim looked down at the floor, his face grim. Meghan noticed an equally distraught look on Jack's face, and she reached across the counter for his hand. "What's wrong?"

Jack, dressed in his uniform, shook his head. "I'm here on business, Meghan," he informed her in a serious voice as her dark eyes widened.

Jack turned to Officer Green, who had risen from his table and was walking toward Jack. "Bradley Green," Jack stated flatly as he looked into Officer Green's eyes.

"What's up, my man?" Officer Green asked jovially. "This is a good surprise. I retired two days ago, and here we are, together again."

Jack narrowed his eyes at Officer Green. "I don't want to say this," he muttered under his breath as Officer Green's expression changed into a look of confusion. "But Bradley Green, you are under arrest. You are being considered a person of interest in the case of Chandler Washington's murder, and I have been instructed to take you down to the station."

Officer Green's jaw dropped. "What?" he shouted. "Are you serious? Jack, come on. Is this a joke?"

Officer Kim silently removed the handcuffs from his

belt and approached Officer Green. Officer Green shoved him away. "Get off of me, Brian Kim," he bellowed. "What on Earth do you think you are doing?

Officer Green tore away from Officer Kim, and Jack grabbed him by the arm. "Irvin!" Officer Green yelled. "Get off of me, or you will be sorry."

Meghan cringed. She had seen Officer Green's temper at the bar when Chandler had antagonized him, and she was worried that he would get out of control.

"Bradley," Jack warned in a stern voice. "Just do this the easy way, man."

Officer Green turned to Cheryl, who was sobbing at the table. "It'll be okay, dear," he told his wife as he held out his wrists. "I know that I am an innocent man. The system will come through for me. Don't you worry."

Officer Kim snapped the handcuffs on Officer Green, and Jack took him by the shoulder. "I'll take you out to the car," he told him.

"Don't you take him!" Cheryl screamed, rising to her feet and dashing to her husband. She beat her delicate fists on Officer Kim's chest. "He is an officer of the law. He is a good man. How dare you accuse him of such a heinous crime?"

Officer Kim looked down at Cheryl. "Ma'am," he said. "You are assaulting an officer of the law. I suggest you take your hands off of me, or we can press charges."

Cheryl took her hands off of Officer Kim, but she did not stop crying. Her wrinkled face grew red, and she collapsed onto the floor as her husband was led outside and put into Officer Kim's car. "Meghan, this is an outrage," she cried as Meghan knelt to join her on the wooden floor. "My husband wouldn't hurt a fly. He talks big, that is true, and he gets riled up sometimes, but I know that he would never do anything as terrible as kill a man."

Meghan pursed her lips. Her heart ached for Cheryl, and she gently stroked Cheryl's back. "It will all be okay," she promised her as Jack walked out of the bakery. "They'll find the answers, Cheryl, I promise. They'll find out who killed Chandler, and then justice will be served."

Cheryl wiped her eyes and hiccuped, her makeup smearing as she retrieved a handkerchief from her handbag and dabbed her face. "They had better," she gasped. "Because my husband is innocent, and I will move Heaven and Earth to prove it."

7

THE NEXT DAY, the sun was shining in Sandy Bay, and despite the cold temperatures, it was a beautiful afternoon. Meghan and Jack decided to take their dogs for a long walk on the beach; Meghan had proposed the idea after hearing that Jack had been working a fifteen hour shift, and she knew he needed some fresh air when his workday was through.

"I'm beat," Jack admitted as he gently tugged on Dash's leather collar. "But I'm glad we did this. Getting outside is perfect, and the sound of the waves is so relaxing."

The dogs ran through the sand dunes. Siesta was chasing Dash, and Fiesta was burrowing into the mix of snow and sand that covered the beach. Meghan loved watching the dogs run around the beach, and she was happy that she and Jack had made it out to enjoy the day.

"I agree," she said, slipping her free hand into Jack's as she held onto Fiesta and Siesta with the other hand. "I can't believe there's been another death in town. It's crazy how much has happened in Sandy Bay since I moved here."

Jack looked down at his sandy boots, his bright blue eyes filled with melancholy. "What's on your mind?" she asked. "You look so upset."

"Of course I am upset," Jack said sharply. "My mentor, my role model, my colleague is locked in a jail cell right now, and to be honest with you, it isn't looking good for him."

Meghan clasped a hand to her mouth. "It isn't?"

Jack shook his head. "No, it isn't. About two dozen witnesses heard Officer Green threatening to kill Chandler after that stupid dart game, and the video footage from the bar shows them arguing. It's bad, Meghan. It looks like he did it. CCTV footage gotten from a convenience store near Chandler's residence shows he was in the area right around when Chandler was killed. "

She furrowed her brow. "But you know he didn't….don't you?"

Jack sighed. He turned away from Meghan and looked out to the horizon. He adjusted the collar on his winter coat and shivered. "I don't," he admitted. "Bradley is a good guy, but he has always been known for his temper. He's yelled at me a bunch of times, and I know that he's gotten physical before with some of the guys at the station. I never thought that he could be a killer, but I do know that when he is in a rage, he can be a scary fellow."

She slipped an arm around Jack's waist. "Just because someone has a temper doesn't mean he is a killer," she insisted weakly.

Jack looked at her. "Chandler died from a dart to his neck," he told her. "The dart hit one of his critical arteries, Meghan. We learn about the arteries in the neck during our police training. We get a refresher course every single year, and we just had our refresher course a month ago. Officer Green would have known exactly where to strike Chandler to kill him."

Meghan pulled Jack close to her. She could sense his frustration, sadness, and concern, and she wanted nothing more than to make everything better for her beloved boyfriend. She stood on her tiptoes and leaned up, just barely tall enough to give Jack a peck on his cheek.

"Hey," she murmured as Jack leaned into her embrace. "I love you. I am here for you."

A wave crashed and the dogs barked playfully. Meghan could taste the salty air, and she waited for Jack's reply. "Jack?"

Jack shook his head. "Sorry," he said. "I was zoned out. What did you say?"

Meghan kissed him again on the cheek. "I said that I

love you," she told him. "I am here for you. I know this is hard, and I know things don't look good for Officer Green, but no matter what you need, I will be here for you."

Meghan was relieved as Jack wrapped an arm around her shoulder and kissed her forehead. "Thanks, babe."

She smiled softly. "I know what could cheer you up," she said to Jack. "Otis is leading a group workout class at the event center today. It's free, and it sounded like fun. Do you want to go? I think Karen will be there, and you know she is always in a good mood. It could help things."

Jack laughed weakly. "I don't know if a workout will solve this problem," he said to Meghan as the smile vanished from her lips. "But if you want me to go, I will. I could probably use a distraction, as well as a good rush of endorphins."

Meghan nodded. "I want you to come with me," she affirmed. "I think it will be good for you. Besides, we've hardly ever worked out together, and it could be a fun new thing for us as a couple."

Jack raised his muscular arms over his head to stretch. "I get a lot of workouts in on the clock at work," he told her as he yawned. "Between chasing criminals and training for my role, I feel like I'm always on my feet." Meghan bit her lip, and Jack continued. "But if you want me there, I'll go. Otis is a buddy of mine, anyway, and it'll be a good time, I'm sure." Meghan wasn't sure if he really meant it or said it to make her happy.

8

MEGHAN DRESSED IN HER CUTEST ATHLETIC ATTIRE for her workout with Jack, a pair of forest green leggings and a matching crew neck sweatshirt. The color brought out her dark eyes, and she skipped confidently down the stairs to meet him when he arrived to pick her up.

"Hey stranger," Meghan teased as she opened the door to Jack's car. "Long time no see."

Jack nodded, a serious look on his face. He was dressed in long gray workout pants and a matching jacket. "Hey," he said distractedly.

"It starts in fifteen minutes, so we are right on time," she told him as he pulled away from the curb. "Karen isn't going to be there after all, but I'm sure Otis will be happy to see us."

They arrived at the event center with five minutes to spare, and Jack parked the car, Meghan walked inside to reserve their spots in the workout class. "Hey, Otis!" she cheerfully greeted her friend as he waved to her from behind the registration desk.

"Hey, yourself," Otis said cheerfully. "I'm glad you're here, Meghan. I think you'll like the class."

"It's honestly perfect timing," Meghan told him as she signed in. "Jack is here too, and he needs something to get the Chandler thing off of his mind."

Otis shuddered. "Chandler," he murmured. "It has me real shaken up that he's gone. I didn't love the guy; you know that he drove me nuts with his carelessness and his antics, but I would never wish ill on the guy."

Meghan nodded. "It is crazy," she agreed. "Jack is pretty torn up about it; Officer Green was arrested, and Jack can't believe that someone he respects so much could do something so terrible."

Otis shrugged. "People do bad things," he said matter of factly. "Sometimes, people we don't expect. I'm sorry to hear Jack is upset. Hopefully this class will help cheer him up."

"That is what I am hoping," she smiled.

"Hi, Otis," Jack greeted as he walked inside to join them. "How are you doing?"

Otis shook his head. "I'm okay, buddy. I am just beside myself about Chandler, but who isn't?"

Jack raised an eyebrow. "Speaking of Chandler," he

began. "Let me ask you, Otis, did you see anything suspicious on the night of the murder? I know you weren't at the party, but you live close to the bar."

Otis scratched his head. "The only weird thing I saw that night was Jamie," he said, referring to the town handyman. "I saw Jamie sprinting down the street around ten at night, and I thought it was strange. He's a weird guy though, so nothing he does surprises me."

Jack frowned. "You saw Jamie Cruise sprinting down the street at ten at night?" he repeated as Otis nodded.

"He was moving real fast, Jack," Otis told him. "Like I said, Jamie is a weird guy, but it did seem odd that he was sprinting around town at that hour."

Jack looked at Meghan, his face serious. "Babe," he said softly. "I need to follow up on this. I am going to have to go."

Meghan opened her mouth, but before she could respond, Jack was gone. "Well, I guess I'm doing the class by myself," she muttered sadly.

Otis grimaced. "He's pretty upset, just like you said. It was all over his face."

She fought back tears, and Otis reached out to gently touch her shoulder. "Hey," he said. "It's okay, Meghan. We'll have a good workout today. What do you want to focus on?"

Meghan sniffled. "I guess I want to work on my coordination," she said. "I'm pretty clumsy, and I need to get better at being more graceful."

Otis stepped back and took a look at Meghan. "May I offer a suggestion?" he asked. "Let's target your overall fitness for this class; improved fitness can improve coordination, and I think if we focus on your holistic movements, you will find that your coordination can improve over time."

Meghan mustered a smile and nodded. "That sounds great," she told him.

Otis wrinkled his forehead in thought. "You know, I have someone who you should meet," he declared. "She's already signed in and in the class, but I think I should pull her out and introduce the pair of you. She's an inspiration, Meghan; she started training with me a few years ago, and her fitness levels have improved drastically. The way she moves is incredible. Do you want to meet her? I think she could be a role model of sorts for you in your own health and fitness journey."

Meghan bit her lip. "I guess so," she said nervously.

Otis chuckled. "She's a sweetheart, Meghan. Let me go grab her."

Otis returned two minutes later. "She's on her way out," he informed Meghan.

"Hey, move your slow bottoms," a familiar voice

screeched. She looked over to see Sally Sheridan, an elderly resident of Sandy Bay, walking down the stairs. She was trying to move past a group of teenagers, and they were in her way. "Move yourselves, young people," Mrs. Sheridan croaked. "I can't wait all day."

Mrs. Sheridan was notorious for her persnickety attitude, but somehow, Meghan had found herself in Mrs. Sheridan's good graces; Mrs. Sheridan had finally warmed to Meghan, and Meghan was thankful to be on her good side.

"There she is," Otis said with a smile as Meghan peered past Mrs. Sheridan.

"Where? Mrs. Sheridan is blocking my view," she told Otis.

"Meghan," Otis laughed. "It's Mrs. Sheridan."

Mrs. Sheridan grinned as she approached Meghan. "I hear you want more of my fitness expertise," she cackled as Meghan's face paled.

Meghan thought back to the self-defense class she had taken a few weeks ago. Mrs. Sheridan had unexpectedly been there, and it turned out that she was a master of kungfu, karate, jujitsu, and taekwondo. Mrs. Sheridan had thrown out Meghan's back during a mock fight, and Meghan had vowed never to workout with Mrs. Sheridan in any capacity ever again.

"I guess the self-defense class wasn't enough for you, Meghan," Mrs. Sheridan laughed. "Well, your sensei is ready to work with you again. I want to take you under my wing, Meghan. Otis tells me that you are going to do the class today, and I want to help you."

Meghan raised an eyebrow. "I'm not sure about that," she told Mrs. Sheridan.

"Oh, don't be a goose," Mrs. Sheridan insisted. "Work out with me. It will be fun."

Meghan made a pleading look at Otis, but he waved her into the class. "Enjoy," he told Meghan.

Meghan begrudgingly followed Mrs. Sheridan into the room. Mrs. Sheridan began to stretch, and she followed her lead. "Good job," Mrs. Sheridan praised as Meghan leaned down to touch her toes. "You'll be just as limber as me in no time."

"You're an old lady with a cane," Meghan thought to herself. "How limber can you be?"

Meghan looked up as Mrs. Sheridan began another stretch. Cheryl Green walked into the room, and the crowd of participants hushed. The silence was awkward, and Meghan felt bad for Cheryl; everyone was staring at her, and Meghan could see she was uncomfortable.

"I'm going to go say hello to her," she told Mrs. Sheridan.

"That's fine," Mrs. Sheridan told her. "But don't talk too much; the more you speak, the more muscles you'll use, and the more muscles you use to chit chat, the less energy you'll have for our little workout."

Meghan stifled the urge to roll her eyes, and she made her way across the room. "Cheryl," she said gently. "How are you holding up?"

Cheryl's eyes were red, but she pasted a smile on her face. "Oh, it's all fine," she told Meghan. "Bradley is innocent, so we have nothing to worry about."

Meghan forced herself to smile back. "That's good to hear," she told Cheryl. "I'm sure you're quite busy, too; Chandler's funeral is this week, and Jack told me that you are going in Bradley's stead?"

Cheryl's eyes narrowed. "Absolutely not," she told Meghan. "Why would I go to that hooligan's funeral?"

Meghan was shocked by Cheryl's strong reaction. "Umm...Bradley worked with him?"

Cheryl shook her head. "My husband may have worked with that scoundrel, but we are not exactly mourning his death," she told Meghan.

"What do you mean?"

Cheryl blinked. "Our relationship with Chandler runs a little deeper than Bradley's work," she informed Meghan.

"Isn't Chandler from California? I thought you and Officer Green were lifelong Sandy Bay residents?" she asked.

Cheryl nodded. "We are," she said. "But three years ago, when Chandler interned at the station here during his master's program, he dated our youngest daughter, Jessie."

Meghan bit her lip. "I didn't know that," she told Cheryl. "Jack didn't say anything about that."

Cheryl shrugged. "It's been awhile," she admitted. "But Chandler came here for a summer, and then, at the end of his internship, he broke our little girl's heart. He told her that he wasn't coming back here, and he ended things with her. We were so angry; Jessie had never been so devastated. It's a hard thing for a parent to see, Meghan."

Meghan nodded. "I can only imagine," she replied. "But he ended up back here? Did he and Jessie get back together?"

"No," Cheryl fumed. "He was assigned a position here by total chance. Jessie was so distraught that she ran away from home."

"She ran away?" she asked, shocked.

"Well, not like a child runs away," Cheryl said. "But she left home and moved to Taiwan to teach English. We haven't seen her in two years. If that jerk hadn't broken her heart and then come back here, she would still be home with us. He hurt her, and then she left home to run away from his memory. It's been terrible for our family."

Meghan could not believe it. She had hoped Officer Green was innocent, but now, it sounded like he had a serious motive. Meghan now understood why Officer Green had been so angry at the bar; he was not only a a man frustrated with his coworker, but a father saddened by the hurt his daughter had experienced.

"I'm so sorry to hear that all happened," she murmured.

Cheryl sighed. "Well, the way I see it now, Chandler got what was coming to him," she said to Meghan with a gleam in her eyes. "He got what he deserved."

9

"SHE'S A HUGE INFLUENCER, MEGHAN! You don't understand. She has over ten thousand followers, and she recommended our lemon tarts to her followers. This is huge."

Meghan laughed. "That sounds like its good news," she told Pamela as they sat together at a little white table in the bakery dining room.

"I don't understand instaphoto," Trudy complained, snapping her watermelon-flavored gum. "We are really missing out by not using Facebook as much as we should, Meghan. I've said it before, and I'll say it again: Facebook is how you connect with the older generations."

Meghan yawned. She was nursing her third cup of coffee, and yet, she was still exhausted. She had been up late talking to Jack on the phone, recounting the conversation she had had with Cheryl Green.

"Jessie left town because of Chandler?" Jack had asked. "I didn't realize that. I knew that they dated, but

I didn't realize it was that serious."

"That's what Cheryl told me," she had said. "And it sounded like Bradley and Cheryl had it out for Chandler."

"It sounds like I need to question her."

"Yeah, I think you should."

Meghan had fallen into a fitful sleep, and she had been rudely awoken by Trudy banging on the bakery door. She had forgotten to set her alarm, and her employees were outside in the cold waiting for her as she groggily wandered to the door.

The little silver bells chimed, and the three women looked up to find Jamie Cruise standing before them. "Hey, ladies," Jamie said in his deep, gruff voice. He was dressed in work overalls that were covered in dirt, and Meghan was afraid his soiled clothes would tarnish the clean floors.

"What can I do for you, Jamie?" she asked.

Jamie shifted awkwardly. "Do you have any work for me?" he asked sheepishly. "Any odd jobs that need done?"

Meghan raised an eyebrow. "I haven't seen you in a few days, Jamie," she asked, thinking back to her conversation with Otis the previous day. She remembered that Otis had seen Jamie running down the street on the night Chandler was murdered, and she was wondering why Jamie had been absent from town the last few days. "Where have you been?"

Jamie's face flushed. "I just ain't been around," he said defensively. "No big deal. Why do you care?"

Meghan bit her lip. "I'm just asking as a friend, Jamie," she told him. "What's the problem?"

Jamie sputtered. "It just ain't your business," he said. "I been doing my things, and that ain't anyone's business."

Meghan's heart began to pound. Jamie was acting strangely, and she had a feeling that something was wrong. "I wonder if Jack has spoken with him yet," she wondered to herself as she stared into Jamie's frantic eyes. "I had better do something."

Meghan pulled out her cell phone. "What are you doing?" Jamie asked, his voice tinged with panic.

"I'm just checking my texts," she lied, seeing the fear on Jamie's face. "I'm waiting on a text from my friend, Jackie. Is that a problem?"

"No!" Jamie yelled in a voice that was just a bit too loud. "It's fine. I don't care."

Meghan rose to her feet and shuffled quickly into the kitchen. She dialed Jack's work number, and he answered on the first ring. "What's up?"

"Jamie Cruise is here," she whispered into the phone. "And he's acting strange. I think you need to come over here. Have you spoken with him yet?"

"No," Jack admitted. "No one has been able to track him down. You said he is there now? At the bakery?"

"Yes," Meghan confirmed. "He's in the dining room. Come over, Jack. I have a bad feeling."

Jack arrived ten minutes later. He was dressed in his uniform, and despite the feeling of panic in her gut, she admired how handsome he was in his Sandy Bay detective attire.

"Thank you for coming," Meghan gushed as she rushed into Jack's arms. "Trudy is keeping Jamie occupied in the kitchen; she is showing him photos on her phone from her trip to Palm Springs, and I haven't heard a peep since they've been back there."

Jack nodded. "Thanks for calling," he said, bending down to kiss her on the lips. "I'm glad we'll have him in custody; Chief Nunan just ordered his arrest based on an interview she did with Otis, per my request, and I am going to take him in right now."

Meghan squeezed Jack's hand. "Good luck," she said.

Jack shook his head. "I'm not quite done with you," he told her apologetically. "I'll need you to come to the station, too."

"Me?" she asked. "Why?"

Jack jerked his chin toward the kitchen. "If Jamie has anything to do with the death of Chandler Washington, I'm gonna need you to testify as to the interaction you two had before you called me," he said. "You said he was acting dodgy and defensive? I'm gonna need that on record."

"Ugh," she replied with a frown. "I don't want to have anything more to do with this case; we talked forever last night about Cheryl Green, and I just want to do my job and go about my day."

"Sorry, honey," Jack said. "That isn't how it works. Now, you stay out of the way while I go apprehend Jamie. You can follow us down to the station, and I'll get your official statements there."

10

"AND WE'RE KEEPING HIM IN CUSTODY UNTIL FURTHER NOTICE."

Stunned, Meghan leaned back in the red leather chair in Jack's office as he sat across from her at his desk. "He's being kept in jail for stealing? Not for murder? Jack, he was acting so shady at the bakery. I can't believe that was all about stealing."

Jack sighed, and Meghan could see how tired he looked. "He confessed to robbery," Jack told her. "When Chief Nunan sat down with him, Jamie admitted that he had gone into Chandler's house to fix the sink, but that Chandler hadn't paid him yet. He stole jewelry from Chandler to make up for the lost profits."

"Why hadn't Chandler paid him?" she asked. "You said Chandler made a boatload of money--even more than the officers."

Jack shrugged. "I can't speak for Chandler," he told her. "But I know what Jamie said. Jamie thought I had brought him in to nail him on stealing Chandler's gold cufflinks from prep school, or something like that. He said he went out of town to sell them, but when he couldn't find a buyer, he came back to town."

Meghan raised an eyebrow. "That sounds a little too convenient," she said. "Chandler is killed, Jamie is seen running away from the direction of the crime, and then, he goes out of town to sell cufflinks? Come on. You should have seen how nervous he was when I asked where he was today, Jack. He looked like he had seen a ghost."

Jack shook his head. "We're looking into his alibi, Meghan," he informed her. "At this point, we're holding him, and that's all I can tell you."

Meghan frowned, and Jack stood from his seat and came around to her side of the desk. "Hey," he said softly, taking Meghan's hands in his. "Let's get out of here. I just worked a seventeen hour shift, and I need a pick me up. Can I take you on a little coffee date?"

Meghan's face burst into a smile. "Yeah," she told her boyfriend. "I guess I'll let you take me out."

Meghan and Jack decided to walk to Spoon, a new coffee shop on the town square. It was bright and airy, and just what Meghan needed; she felt cheerful immediately upon entering, and she happily ordered a matcha latte, a drink she had grown to like after Karen had recommended it a few weeks ago.

The couple settled onto a soft yellow couch in the corner. They held hands, and she enjoyed the quality time with Jack; it had been a few weeks since they had enjoyed a proper date, and she always craved one-on-one time with him. Jack's hand drifted down to Meghan's knee, and his touch sent shivers down her back.

"Not to ruin our date, but tell me, what do you think of the case?" Jack asked as Meghan sighed.

"I really don't want to talk about Chandler Washington, or anything else pertaining to this mess," she told Jack, folding her arms across her chest. "I just want to spend some time with my man."
Jack nodded. "I'm sorry," he told her. "I just can't stop thinking about it. When I spoke with Cheryl Green this morning, there was just something about her eyes that tipped me off. I have a pretty good gut instinct, and she is someone I am keeping an eye on."

Meghan bit her lip. "I feel bad for Cheryl, but I agree, I feel like something was off with her when we chatted," she told Jack.

Meghan's phone rang, and she saw Otis' name flash across the screen. "It's Otis," she told Jack. "He had some great tips for me when I took his class, and I think we're going to start training together more often. Let me answer this quickly."

Meghan rose from the couch and walked toward the vestibule. "Otis," she answered cheerfully. "How are you doing?"

"I'm good, Meghan," Otis said. "Hey, I was thinking about our conversation from the other day, and I think i may have a solution for your coordination problems."

"Oh, really?" she asked eagerly. "You're joking."

"Nope," Otis replied. "I was wracking my brain late last night, and I am sure I have a solution...or at least, something that will help. Any chance you're free later? You could come over to my place for a few. I also have that Zumba DVD back from my neighbor."

"Yes!" she cried. "That would be awesome. I'm grabbing dinner with Jackie tonight, but we'll swing by beforehand. Is that alright? Around eight?"

"Great," Otis agreed. "I'll see you soon."

Meghan walked back inside and sat back down. "What did Otis want?" Jack asked.

"He has the Zumba DVD I wanted," she said, embarrassed to admit that Otis was going to help her with her terrible coordination. "Jackie and I are going to stop by his place and get it before we go to dinner."

"That's cool, babe," he told her. "I hear his house is so nice; he used it to counsel at-risk juveniles and to run his weight loss group, and from what I've been told, it's a pretty sweet place."

Meghan smiled. "I'm excited to see it. I'll text you when Jackie and I leave and let you know how it went."

"That sounds like a plan, babe," he said with a smile. "I can't wait to hear how it goes."

11

"AND THIS IS THE HANGOUT SPACE," Otis announced as he led Meghan and Jackie into his cavernous half-finished basement. "This is where I do some of my community work. It isn't fancy, but it's a good sized space, and it's comfy enough."

Jackie looked around. "This is huge," she exclaimed. "You could fit quite a crowd in here!"

Otis laughed. "I love hosting," he told her. "Meghan, we might even do some of our personal training here. I have a set of weights in the back, and it's a great private space for a workout."

Meghan looked over to the corner and saw a bag of golf clubs. "Are those Calloway clubs?" she asked.

Otis nodded. "They are," he confirmed. "I'm impressed you know the brand. Are you a big golfer?"

Meghan shook her head and giggled. "You've seen me in action; I'm not quite sporty," she told Otis. "But my daddy loves golf. He used to let me drive the cart when he went."

Meghan removed one of the clubs from the bag, imagining her girlhood days driving around the golf course with her father. She ran her hands up and down the smooth silver club, and then realized the head was missing. "It's broken," she told Otis. "What happened?"

Otis sighed. "Chandler," he said. "He borrowed them for an outing with his friends, and when he returned them, well…."

Jackie shook her head. "That would make me so mad," she said. "You can't take someone's things and then return them broken."

Otis shrugged. "Chandler did what he wanted," he said to Jackie. "Oddly enough, though, I miss the guy; he was a terrible neighbor, but in a funny way, I miss him. There's no one around to break my stuff anymore."

Meghan laughed softly. "That's terrible," she teased.

"I'm just kidding," Otis said. "Really, though, so sad what happened to him."

"It is," Jackie agreed, pushing her newly-trimmed brown bangs out of her eyes. "He was a cutie, that's for sure."

Sick of discussing Chandler and the murder, Meghan

changed the subject. "So, what was this idea you had, Otis?" she asked. "How can I improve my coordination?"

"Darts," he said matter of factly.

"Darts?" she said in disgust. "After what happened with Chandler, I can't even think about playing darts; all I can imagine is Officer Green and Chandler fighting over the dart tournament at the bar."

"Oh, come on, Meghan," Otis said. "There are so many benefits. Darts can improve coordination and focus, and it's fun to play. Come on! I have a massive board in my backyard. Let's play a round, just to try it. What do you think? Jackie? Are you in?"

Jackie shrugged. "As long as it won't mess up my nails," she said, batting her eyelashes flirtatiously at Otis. "I'll do it."

"Fine," she huffed. "Lead the way, Otis."

Otis led the women upstairs and outside. They all shuddered when the cold air hit their skin, but then, Otis turned on a heat lamp.

"Gotta warm up the fingers," Otis joked as he lit the heat lamp, and Meghan was grateful for the sudden burst of warm air.

"How did you start playing darts?" Jackie asked as Otis stretched his arms and shook out his hands.

"Actually, it was Chandler who introduced me to the game," Otis announced. "I had some guys over a couple of years ago to hang out, and Chandler brought a small board over. I got hooked, and I ended up buying this board for myself a few weeks later."

Meghan and Jackie admired the enormous dart board that hung to the right of the garage. "This is a nice set, isn't it?" Meghan asked.

Otis nodded, his eyes bright. "It's top-class," he told her. "Well, it was; Chandler borrowed a bunch of my darts and never returned them, and now, my set is incomplete. It's a bummer; the last set he lost was a collectible. I guess I just had too much faith that he would learn his lesson each time he lost my stuff, and he always proved me wrong…"

"So, if the set is incomplete, can we still play now?" Jackie asked.

"Of course," Otis said. "I have a cheap set that I bought last week. One dart is missing, but we still have three out of the four darts."

"Did Chandler lose the missing one?" Meghan asked.

Otis wrinkled his nose. "I can't remember how it was lost," he sighed. "Sometimes the darts just disappear before my eyes. It was probably my fault this time."

Meghan nodded. "Gotcha," she said. "Well, let's get started."

The three lined up. Jackie threw her dart first, and she completely missed the board. Her dart landed in the yard. "Next time!" Otis told her. "Meghan, you are up."

Meghan hit the dart board, but she was nowhere near the target. "Whoops," she shrugged.

"That's okay," Otis said. "My turn."

Otis picked up his dart, and without hesitation, he hurled it toward the dart board. It struck the target directly in the center. "Bullseye," he murmured as Meghan stared in awe.

"You're pretty good with those darts," Meghan exclaimed. "What a natural. You hit it dead on."

Otis smirked. "It's pretty easy for me," he agreed. "I'm pretty naturally inclined, but I took a few classes, and I think I'm getting good enough to compete professionally."

Meghan could not tear her gaze from the dart sitting in the middle of the blood red target. Otis' aim had been perfect; even watching the officers and IT guys at the retirement party, Meghan had never seen such an accurate throw before.

"Say," Meghan began slowly. "Did you know Bradley Green, Otis?"

"Bradley Green?" Otis repeated. "The police officer?

Yeah, I knew him. He and my dad were good friends back in the day."

Meghan pursed her lips. "Did I miss you at his retirement party? I don't think I saw you there?"

"Oh?" Otis replied carefully. "I was there for a bit."

"What time?" Meghan asked. "I was there most of the night and didn't see you."

Otis' eyes flashed, and Meghan leaned over to Jackie. "Take my phone and call Jack," she whispered. "Go now. Tell him I think I may know who murdered Chandler Washington."

12

"WHAT ARE YOU GIRLS TALKING ABOUT?" Otis asked, stepping closer to Meghan and Jackie as Jackie turned and dashed away.

"Nothing," she sputtered. "Just girl talk."

"Oh, fill me in," he pleaded. "What did you say to Jackie, Meghan?"

Meghan stared up at Otis. He was taller and bigger than her, and she felt her heart beating furiously in her chest. "It was nothing, Otis," she lied. "Truly, I just asked if she wanted to see a chick flick later."

Otis backed down. "Oh, okay," he said, smiling widely at Meghan. "Haha, I was only teasing anyway. Let's get back to our dart game, shall we?"

Meghan stared at the long, thick dart in Otis' hand. The tail was painted scarlet, and the tip was sharper than a knife. She gulped. "Sure," she replied, hoping that Jack would arrive soon. "Let's play again."

Otis gestured to the board. "Your turn," he told her. "Where did Jackie go? Didn't she go before you?"

Meghan shook her head. "She had to...use the restroom," she told him. "I'll go for her."

Meghan threw the dart and missed. She threw another one, missing again, and Otis chuckled. "Relax, Meghan," he urged her. "You seem nervous. Everything alright?"

Meghan remembered her conversation with Jack about Chandler's death. Chandler had been killed by a dart that hit one of his arteries in the perfect place. As she watched Otis hurl another dart and hit the target perfectly, she felt her face break out in a hot sweat. "I'm fine," she told him. "Just fine."

Just then, Meghan heard a familiar voice, and her heart leapt with joy. "Otis Barber," Jack's deep voice called out from across the lawn. "Stop right there and put the dart down."

Otis turned around and obeyed, letting the dart fall. His eyes were large as he eyed the gun in Jack's hand. "Jack? What's up? What are you doing?"

Jack walked to Otis and placed him in handcuffs. "You are under arrest for the murder of Chandler Washington," he declared. "And I am taking you in."

One week later, Meghan, Pamela, and Trudy were sitting in front of Meghan's laptop as they updated the bakery website together. Meghan had gotten more tips about SEO from Molly Owens, and the trio was completing the update as they munched on fresh muffins.

"There. It's done." Meghan said with satisfaction as the page loaded. "We did it, ladies."

"Yes!" Pamela squealed. "Okay, now will you tell us what happened?"

Meghan laughed. "Fine, fine," she agreed. "Now that our work is all done, we can chit chat. Where should I start?"

Trudy shook her head. "Tell us what happened when Jack took Otis in," she demanded. "You've been tight-lipped all week, and we know you know what is going on."

Meghan nodded. "I've been under orders not to say anything," she explained. "But the full story is hitting the news later, so I can talk about it now."

Pamela leaned in. "Tell us everything."

Meghan sighed. "It's a mess," she admitted. "Otis' fingerprints were found on the dart that killed Chandler."

"No!" Pamela moaned. "He is so nice and so cute. How can he be a killer? Ugh, this stinks!"

Meghan shook her head. "There is more," she declared. "Otis surrendered the security cameras he keeps in his backyard and around his house. It turns out that the dart that killed Chandler was one that he threw by accident. He came home after a few drinks at the retirement party, and he was warming up for his nightly game. He tossed the dart, and he had no idea it killed Chandler. The tapes prove it; Otis couldn't have known."

Trudy gasped. "Seriously?"

Meghan nodded. "It's been determined that it was accidental manslaughter. Otis didn't mean to kill Chandler. It was a total accident."

Trudy shook her head. "That is awful," she said.

Meghan hung her head. "There is more," she told them. "The tapes that Otis gave up? Well, they showed Officer Green committing a terrible deed of his own."

"No," Pamela gasped. "What did he do?"

Meghan leaned in. "He was cheating on his wife," she said sadly. "And he was on the way to meet his mistress when the tapes caught him near Chandler's house. That's why he was around the scene of the crime."

Pamela's eyes grew wide. "Oh my goodness," she lamented. "That is terrible."

Meghan nodded. "It's been a sad week in Sandy Bay for a lot of reasons," she agreed. "But, I have some good news for us."

"What is it?" Trudy asked. "I think we need some cheering up after all of this bad news. Chandler dead, Otis charged with manslaughter, and Bradley a cheater...well, what is the good news?"

Meghan could not keep the grin off of her face. "That influencer you mentioned last week?" she said to Pamela. "Well, her love of my lemon tarts got around to the local news station. They are going to do a news piece on the tarts and the bakery, and the anchors are coming over here tonight to shoot some footage for a feature on tomorrow's evening news!"

Pamela shrieked. "That's amazing, Meghan!" she

cried.

"Congratulations, dear," Trudy said. "You must be thankful for such a good piece of news. It's well deserved."

Meghan nodded. She was tired from the events of the week, but as she looked around the bakery, at the business she had built from the ground up, she beamed. "It is a good piece of news," Meghan told them. "In fact, it is truly sweet."

The End

Afterword

Thank you for reading Lemon Tarts and Fiery Darts! I really hope you enjoyed reading it as much as I had writing it!

If you have a minute, please consider leaving a review on Amazon.

Many thanks in advance for your support!

MUFFINS AND COFFINS CHAPTER 1 SNEEK PEEK

Meghan smiled sleepily as she awoke to the sound of birds chirping outside of her open bedroom windows. She sighed, inhaling the sweet, floral scent of the honey locust growing just below her second story apartment, thrilled that winter had finally ended and spring was making its first appearances in Sandy Bay, her adopted hometown in the Pacific Northwest.

Still enjoying the sounds of the morning, Meghan snuggled further beneath her comforter. She reached over and picked up Fiesta and Siesta, her tiny twin dogs, and piled them both on her chest. "Good morning, babies," Meghan murmured as she gave them each a kiss on the forehead. "It's finally the weekend. Your mama only works a few hours this morning, so perhaps we will go for a little walk on the beach later."

Meghan giggled as Siesta licked her on the nose. Fiesta followed suit, and Meghan scratched her behind the ears. She inhaled, and caught the smell of fresh muffins coming from the bakery downstairs.

"It smells like Trudy is off to a great start this morning," Meghan said aloud, picturing her trusted middle-aged employee, Trudy, dressed in her apron and preparing the muffins. "She is such a rockstar on the morning shifts."

Meghan took another deep breath, detecting a hint of lavender as she closed her eyes. "I hope she is making the lemon-lavender muffins today. Those have been selling out like crazy."

Meghan lounged for a few more minutes, and then, as she heard Pamela, a local teenager she had hired a few months ago, greet Trudy downstairs, she peeled herself out of bed. She gathered her long, dark hair into a high ponytail and slipped into a pair of green cargo pants. She tied her apron on over her outfit and quickly surveyed herself in the mirror as she walked to her door. Meghan preferred a natural look; she typically did not wear a lot of makeup, and she smiled at her reflection as she passed the mirror.

At twenty-eight, Meghan felt more beautiful than ever, inside and out; she had raven-colored hair that fell down her back in soft waves, a light smattering of coffee-colored freckles across her small nose, and enormous dark eyes with long lashes. She was also the founder and owner of Truly Sweet, a bakery that had quickly gained popularity in its first year of business, and she was proud of the hard work that had turned the bakery into a massive success.
Meghan also had a serious relationship with Jack, a detective, and she fell in love with him more and more every day. She had a good relationship with her family, who lived in Texas, and she had developed several meaningful, close friendships in Sandy Bay.

Everything had been falling in place for Meghan, and she was happier than ever. It would soon be her one-year anniversary of moving to Sandy Bay, and she was hoping to throw a party to celebrate. She had been weighing the idea for several weeks, and she was ready to share it with Trudy and Pamela. After brushing her teeth and applying a thin layer of lip gloss, Meghan walked downstairs and into the kitchen, excited to tell her employees about the party.

"Good morning, ladies," Meghan greeted them as she tucked a loose strand of dark hair back into her ponytail. "I have something I would like to share with you today!"

Pamela turned to Meghan, her nose wrinkled in disgust. She held out her phone to show Meghan the screen. "Does it have anything to do with this?"

Meghan peered at Pamela's phone. It was opened to the bakery's Instagram page. "Why are you showing me the Instagram page, Pamela? I told you that I liked the last few pictures you posted."

Pamela shook her head. "Look closer. I'm in the private messaging section."

Meghan squinted. "It's a message about a funeral service," she gasped. "They want to know if Truly Sweet sells coffins and provides funeral services."

Pamela nodded. "We've gotten five messages from different accounts this morning," she explained, her face filled with confusion. "When I message the accounts back, they vanish off of social media. It seems like a prank."

Trudy stepped forward, her arms crossed over her chest. "The same thing has been happening with our Facebook page," she told Meghan. "It's the strangest thing; we've been getting message after message about the bakery offering funeral services."

Meghan bit her bottom lip, feeling deflated. She had wanted to bring up the idea for the party, but now, it was evident that this issue needed to take priority over the celebration.

"What should we do, Meghan? Should we ask Jack to check this out?" Pamela asked earnestly. "He's a detective. He can track down whoever is pranking us!"

Meghan laughed. "It doesn't seem like an emergency," she patiently said. "But, I will give Jack a call. This is starting to feel like harassment, especially if it is coming from two forms of social media."

Meghan pulled her phone out of her pocket and gasped as she unlocked the main screen. A chain of emails popped up, each with the subject line FUNERAL SERVICES.

"What is it?" Trudy asked, peering over Meghan's shoulder. "Oh no! It's the same thing. Why are people asking us for funeral services? We are a bakery."

Pamela's eyes grew wide. "I'm creeped out, Meghan," she told her boss. "Call Jack right now!"

Meghan paused for a moment, trying to make sense of the emails and messages. "Do you think someone is pulling an April Fool's Day prank?" she asked her employees. "I know it's a week past April Fool's, but what if…?"

Trudy pursed her lips. "I don't think so," she answered. "In Sandy Bay, no one really takes April Fool's Day seriously; I know they do some silly activities at the high school, but no one takes it too far."

"Yeah," Pamela agreed. "A couple of my friends left balloons and silly string in a locker, but no one would be rude to businesses in town. That would be so dumb."

Meghan cleared her phone screen and began dialing Jack's number, eager to hear his opinion on the matter. "Ugh, it went straight to Jack's voicemail. I'll have to call him later."

Trudy put her hands on her hips. "Well, we have about fifteen orders of muffins to fill before you are off for the afternoon," she informed Meghan. "Why don't we get started? Pamela and I will keep an eye on the social media pages for now, and you can pass along the word to Jack when you get ahold of him."

"That sounds good," Meghan agreed as she stepped

over to the sink to wash her hands.

The three ladies baked two batches of muffins, trying to forget about the strange inquiries they had received. When the little silver bells attached to the front door chimed, Meghan sent Pamela out front. "Our first customer of the morning," Meghan said cheerfully as she shooed Pamela into the dining room. "Go wait on them, Pamela."

Pamela returned a moment later, her face pale and her hands shaking. "What is the matter?" Meghan asked, seeing the shock on her face.

"It's an old man," Pamela stammered. "And he asked if we sell coffins."

-

You can order your copy of **Muffins and Coffins** at any good online retailer.

A SANDY BAY 13 COZY MYSTERY

Muffins and Coffins

AMBER CREWES

ALSO BY AMBER CREWES

The Sandy Bay Cozy Mystery Series

Apple Pie and Trouble

Brownies and Dark Shadows

Cookies and Buried Secrets

Doughnuts and Disaster

Éclairs and Lethal Layers

Finger Foods and Missing Legs

Gingerbread and Scary Endings

Hot Chocolate and Cold Bodies

Ice Cream and Guilty Pleasures

Jingle Bells and Deadly Smells

King Cake and Grave Mistakes

Lemon Tarts and Fiery Darts

Muffins and Coffins

Newsletter Signup

Want **FREE** COPIES OF FUTURE **AMBER CREWES** BOOKS, FIRST NOTIFICATION OF NEW RELEASES, CONTESTS AND GIVEAWAYS?

GO TO THE LINK BELOW TO SIGN UP TO THE NEWSLETTER!

www.AmberCrewes.com/cozylist

Manufactured by Amazon.ca
Bolton, ON

14271565R00058